The Twelve Days of Christmas

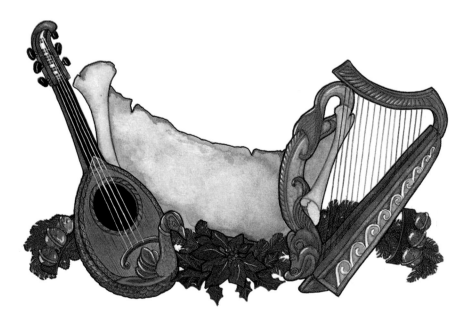

The Twelve

For Lia

JAN BRETT

Days of Christmas

G. P. Putnam's Sons

An Imprint of Penguin Group (USA) Inc.

n the first day of Christmas

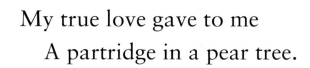

My true love gave to me
    A partridge in a pear tree.

Buon

On the second day of Christmas
My true love gave to me

Two turtledoves,
    And a partridge in a pear tree.

On the third day of Christmas
My true love gave to me
Three French hens,

Two turtledoves,
   And a partridge in a pear tree.

On the fourth day of Christmas
My true love gave to me
Four colly birds,

Three French hens,
Two turtledoves,
    And a partridge in a pear tree.

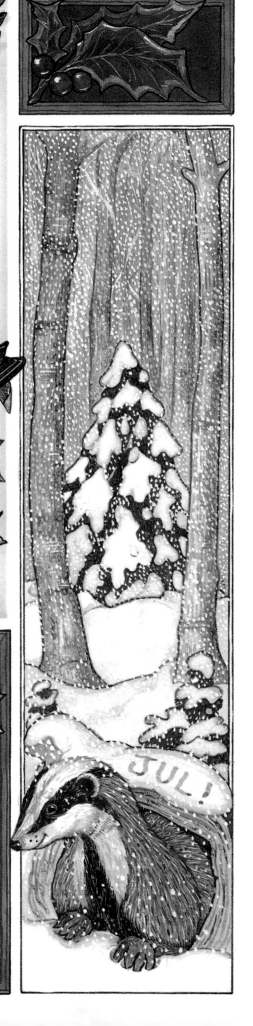

On the fifth day of Christmas
My true love gave to me
    Five gold rings,
    Four colly birds,

Three French hens,
Two turtledoves,
    And a partridge in a pear tree.

KERSTDAGEN

On the sixth day of Christmas
My true love gave to me
Six geese a-laying,
Five gold rings,

Four colly birds,
Three French hens,
Two turtledoves,
    And a partridge in a pear tree.

СЧАСТЛИВОГО

On the seventh day of Christmas
My true love gave to me
    Seven swans a-swimming,
    Six geese a-laying,
    Five gold rings,

Four colly birds,
Three French hens,
Two turtledoves,
    And a partridge in a pear tree.

РОЖДЕСТВА!

On the eighth day of Christmas
My true love gave to me
  Eight maids a-milking,
  Seven swans a-swimming,
  Six geese a-laying,

Five gold rings,
Four colly birds,
Three French hens,
Two turtledoves,
   And a partridge in a pear tree.

On the ninth day of Christmas
My true love gave to me
   Nine drummers drumming,
   Eight maids a-milking,
   Seven swans a-swimming,
   Six geese a-laying,

Five gold rings,
Four colly birds,
Three French hens,
Two turtledoves,
    And a partridge in a pear tree.

On the tenth day of Christmas
My true love gave to me
    Ten pipers piping,
    Nine drummers drumming,
    Eight maids a-milking,
    Seven swans a-swimming,

Six geese a-laying,
Five gold rings,
Four colly birds,
Three French hens,
Two turtledoves,
    And a partridge in a pear tree.

Chridheil

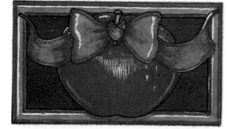

On the eleventh day of Christmas
My true love gave to me
   Eleven ladies dancing,
   Ten pipers piping,
   Nine drummers drumming,
   Eight maids a-milking,
   Seven swans a-swimming,

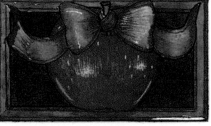

Six geese a-laying,
Five gold rings,
Four colly birds,
Three French hens,
Two turtledoves,
    And a partridge in a pear tree.

On the twelfth day of Christmas
My true love gave to me
    Twelve lords a-leaping,
    Eleven ladies dancing,
    Ten pipers piping,
    Nine drummers drumming,
    Eight maids a-milking,

Seven swans a-swimming,
Six geese a-laying,
Five gold rings,
Four colly birds,
Three French hens,
Two turtledoves,
    And a partridge in a pear tree.

New Year!

A Brief History

The Twelve Days of Christmas are the days linking Christmas on December 25 and the Epiphany on January 6, when the three Magi offered the first Christmas presents—gold, frankincense, and myrrh. These days were declared a religious holiday by the Council of Tours in 567. It became a time for noble and peasant alike to put work aside and enjoy a holiday of feasting, celebration, and sharing with others. It was considered bad luck to enter someone's house empty-handed.

The ancient counting song named for this religious holiday is actually quite pagan in tone and is the only carol we know that celebrates, in the form of a list, the Christmas tradition of gift giving. It is said to date back to a thirteenth-century manuscript in the Library of Trinity College, Cambridge, England. The carol appeared in print for the first time in a children's book entitled *Mirth Without Mischief*, published in London about 1780.

"The Twelve Days of Christmas" became popular as a game song—usually played at a large gathering of children and adults on the Twelfth Night, just before the eating of mince pie. With the company seated around the room, the leader of the game began by singing the first-day lines, which were then repeated by each of the company in turn. Then the first-day lines were repeated with the addition of the second-day lines by the leader, and this was repeated by all in turn. This continued until all the lines of the twelve days were repeated by everyone. If anyone missed a line, they would have to forfeit something of theirs to the group.

THE TWELVE DAYS

VERSES 1-4

English traditional carol

1. On the first* day of Christ-mas my
2. On the se-cond* day of Christ-mas my

true love gave to me a
true love gave to me

four col-ly birds, three French hens, two tur-tle-doves,
four three — two

and a par-tridge in a pear tree.

VERSES 5-12

5. On the fifth* day of Christ-mas my true love gave to me twelve lords a-leap-ing,
6. On the sixth* day of Christ-mas my true love gave to me twelve

*Sing appropriate number of day, and then cut from † to appropriate boxed number.

OF CHRISTMAS